"Shadows of Dupo is a captivating and atmospheric tale that had me hooked from the very first page. The way the author skillfully weaves together the stories of Cole, the troubled graffiti artist, and Officer Harris, the embodiment of corruption, is simply masterful. The characters are richly developed, and the tension between light and darkness is palpable throughout the entire narrative. It's a thrilling and thought-provoking read that will leave you pondering the power of art, justice, and the choices we make." - Sarah R.

"I couldn't put this book down! The story of Cole and Officer Harris is a gripping and haunting journey into the depths of a town consumed by shadows. The author's descriptions bring the streets of Dupo to life, painting a vivid backdrop for the characters' struggles. The themes of resilience, friendship, and the transformative power of art are beautifully explored. If you're a fan of dark, atmospheric tales with a touch of the supernatural, this book is a must-read." - Mark L.

"Shadows of Dupo is a triumph of storytelling. The author's ability to create a vivid sense of place, drawing readers into the gritty and haunting world of Dupo, is truly remarkable. The characters, especially Cole and Officer Harris, are complex and flawed, making their journeys all the more compelling. This book delves deep into themes of corruption, redemption, and the battle between light and darkness. It's a dark and atmospheric read that will leave you both breathless and introspective." - Jennifer M.

SHADOWS

OF

DUPO

A DANCE OF ART AND CORRUPTION

A story by

J.W. JARVIS

Chapter 1: The Enigmatic Town of Dupo

Chapter 2: Echoes of Art and Shadows

Chapter 3: Dance of Shadows

Chapter 4: Whispers of the Bluffs

Chapter 5: Shadows Unleashed

Chapter 6: A New Dawn

Chapter 7: Unveiling the Ghostly Entity

Chapter 8: The Haunted Caves

Chapter 9: Confronting Officer Harris

Chapter 10: Battle in the Underground Chamber

Chapter 11: The Triumph of Light

Chapter 12: Epilogue: A Transformed Dupo

Thank you for purchasing this book!

Check out my other stories coming soon!

This story was written for my children:

Ashlee, Alizjah, Myla, Tristan

I will always love you!

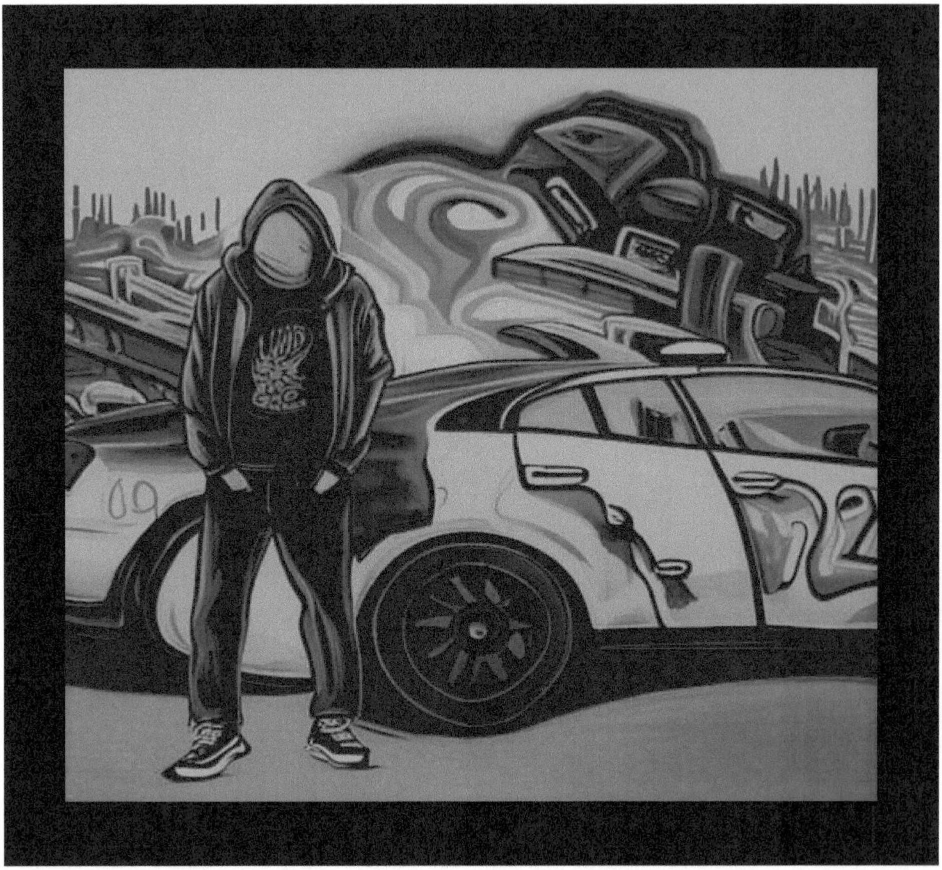

Prologue:

Whispers in the Night

In the heart of Dupo, where the railroad tracks snaked through the town's core, a group of graffiti artists gathered. They were the dreamers, the rebels who sought to breathe life into the forgotten corners, infusing the urban landscape with vibrant colors and imaginative designs. Among them was Cole, a young artist with a restless spirit and a troubled past.

As the moon cast a pale glow upon the deserted streets, the artists created their masterpieces, their paint cans rattling like musical notes in the night. But in the depths of their artistry, they unknowingly awakened something far more sinister—an entity that had long been imprisoned within the town's forgotten history.

As the artists applied their final strokes, a chill wind whispered through the alleyways, carrying with it a sense of foreboding. The air crackled with a restless energy, and the ghostly presence stirred, drawn to the creativity and passion that permeated the air.

And then, in a flicker of ethereal light, the ghostly entity materialized before them, its form both beautiful and terrifying. Eyes filled with sorrow and longing surveyed the artists, a silent plea for redemption emanating from its translucent figure. The artists stood frozen, their hearts pounding, as the ghostly entity beckoned them closer, silently imploring them to uncover the truth that lay hidden within Dupo's dark past.

Little did they know that their encounter with the ghostly entity would set in motion a series of events that would test their resilience, unravel the secrets of the town, and pit them against the forces of darkness that had long haunted Dupo's streets.

CHAPTER ONE: THE ENIGMATIC TOWN OF DUPO

The night sky hung heavy over the small train town of Dupo, casting a cloak of darkness upon its streets. Nestled in the heartland of America, Dupo was a place where time seemed to stand still, frozen in the nostalgic embrace of the 1990s. A once-thriving railroad community, it now whispered its forgotten tales through rusty tracks and dilapidated buildings.

In the shadows of this forgotten town, a group of nocturnal artists and musicians found solace in the vibrant colors and beats that echoed through their restless souls. The graffiti-covered walls became their canvas, and the dimly lit streets their stage. Each night, they brought life to the desolation, transforming it into a haven of creativity.

Among them was Cole, a lanky and enigmatic graffiti artist with an insatiable thirst for adventure. His fingertips danced with spray cans, weaving intricate tales of rebellion and beauty across the urban landscape. Cole's art was an expression of his untamed spirit, a reflection of the darkness that lurked within him.

But tonight, an eerie sense of foreboding settled upon Dupo. Whispers floated through the air, carrying tales of a ghostly presence that haunted the town. The ghost, said to be an entity from the depths of despair, preyed upon those who dared to venture out after the moon rose high.

Cole had heard the rumors, dismissing them as the tales of superstitious minds. Yet, as he made his way to the abandoned train yard, where the artists often gathered, an unsettling chill coursed through his veins. The faint sound of a distant train horn added to the haunting atmosphere, causing him to quicken his pace.

Arriving at the train yard, Cole found his fellow artists already immersed in their creations. Neon hues danced on the walls, casting an ethereal glow upon the surrounding darkness. The music, a fusion of heavy guitar riffs and electronic beats, reverberated through the air, mingling with the distant clank of metal.

The night was alive with energy, yet an unspoken unease hung in the air. The artists worked with a sense of urgency, their movements fueled by an invisible force, as if time itself were running out. They sought to immortalize their stories on these walls, as if driven by a shared fear that their days were numbered.

Suddenly, the peace was shattered by the blaring sirens of police cars, slicing through the night like a knife. Blue and red lights painted the scene, casting an ominous glow on the artists and their masterpieces. The police, wary of the graffiti artists and their defiance of the status quo, had arrived to enforce their version of order.

Chaos erupted as the artists scrambled to escape the clutches of the law, seeking refuge in the shadows and alleyways. Cole's heart raced as he darted away, his footsteps echoing in the deserted streets. He knew the consequences of capture, the price he would pay for his art.

But as he turned a corner, a figure materialized before him, seemingly out of thin air. A ghastly apparition, its form flickering in the pale moonlight, stood between Cole and his escape. The entity's hollow eyes locked onto his, piercing his soul with a silent plea for help.

Fear gripped Cole's heart, his breath caught in his throat. The ghostly figure reached out with a translucent hand, beckoning him closer. Cole hesitated, torn between the terror that gripped him and an inexplicable sense of compassion.

In that moment, as the police sirens blared in the distance and the ghostly entity stood before him, Cole realized that his journey had only just begun. The haunting presence that lurked within the depths of Dupo was no ordinary ghost. It held secrets and a malevolence that threatened to consume him and everything he held dear. As the specter's pale hand trembled in the night air, Cole made his choice. He extended his own hand, his fate entwined with the ghostly entity, and took his first step into the heart of the horror that lay hidden within the train town of Dupo. Little did he know, he was about to unveil a darkness that would test the limits of his courage, his friendships, and his very existence.

CHAPTER TWO: ECHOES OF ART AND SHADOWS

Cole's heart pounded in his chest as he stood face to face with the ghostly entity. The pale moonlight reflected off the spectre's translucent form, casting an otherworldly glow around them. A shiver ran down his spine, but an inexplicable connection drew him closer to the enigmatic presence.

A sudden gust of wind carried whispers through the air, like the town held its breath, awaiting the unfolding of an otherworldly tale. Cole extended his trembling hand, feeling a surge of electricity course through his fingertips as they brushed against the spectral figure.

"I... I want to help you," Cole stammered, his voice barely audible. The ghostly entity's eyes flickered, as if it understood his words. It nodded ever so slightly before dissolving into the night, leaving behind an eerie sense of anticipation. You could still feel the energy in the air. Before Cole knew what had happened he thought to himself "this is real".

As Cole tried to comprehend what had just transpired, the sound of approaching footsteps jolted him back to reality. He retreated into the shadows, where he spotted a petite figure emerging from the darkness. It was Maya, a talented graffiti artist with a mischievous smile that mirrored Cole's own. Maya possessed an uncanny ability to bring her colorful imagination to life on the walls, infusing her art with a touch of whimsy and magic.

"Did you see that? The ghost?" Maya whispered, her voice laced with a mixture of awe and fear.

Cole nodded, still reeling from the encounter. "It was... surreal. But it needs our help. I can feel it."

Maya's eyes widened with a mix of curiosity and determination. "Then let's find out how to help it. Together."

With a newfound sense of purpose, Cole and Maya embarked on a quest to unravel the mystery that haunted their beloved town. They spent their days scouring the library, poring over dusty books and forgotten folklore. They even talked with locals, whose memories clung to the past like cobwebs in an attic. Slowly, a story began to take shape, woven from whispers and long-forgotten tales.

Meanwhile, in the shadows of Dupo, a pet dog named Scraps became an unwitting witness to the unfolding horrors. Scraps, a scruffy mutt with a heart full of loyalty, had been faithfully following Cole and Maya during their nocturnal escapades. His presence brought a touch of warmth and companionship amidst the darkness that enveloped the town.

As the trio delved deeper into the ghost's story, they discovered a connection to one of the police officers patrolling the streets of Dupo. Officer Harris, a weathered and gruff figure, was known for his strict enforcement of the law. His demeanor held a menacing edge, hinting at a hidden darkness that went beyond his role as a law enforcer.

Their investigation unearthed rumors of Officer Harris's involvement in shady dealings, abuse of power, and his tendency to target the very artists and musicians who breathed life into the town. They became convinced that his connection to the ghostly entity held the key to unlocking the dark forces at play.

    With their evidence gathered, Cole, Maya, and Scraps decided to confront Officer Harris. They chose a moonlit night, when the shadows whispered their secrets, and met him near the abandoned train yard. As they approached, the flickering glow of a cigarette revealed Officer Harris's presence.

"You kids should know better than to meddle in things you don't understand," Officer Harris sneered, his voice dripping with disdain.

"We know what you've been doing, Harris," Cole retorted, his voice trembling with a mixture of defiance and fear. "We won't let you harm this town any longer."

Officer Harris's eyes narrowed, a malicious grin spreading across his face. "You have no idea what you're up against, but you're about to find out."

In that moment, a sinister presence stirred in the night air, as if the very shadows were coiling around them, tightening their grip. The stage was set for a battle between the forces of creativity and the darkness that threatened to engulf them all.

As Officer Harris reached for his weapon, Cole, Maya, and Scraps braced themselves for a confrontation that would test not only their mettle but also the bonds of friendship and the resilience of their spirits. The showdown had begun, and the true horrors of Dupo were about to be revealed.

Chapter 3: Dance of Shadows

The moon hung high in the night sky, casting an ethereal glow over the abandoned train yard. Cole, Maya, and Scraps stood their ground, facing Officer Harris, whose malevolent gaze bore into their souls. The air crackled with tension as the echoes of their confrontation danced through the desolate landscape.

Before anyone could make a move, a bloodcurdling scream pierced the night. The trio turned toward the source of the sound and gasped in horror. Amongst the flickering shadows, they saw a lifeless body sprawled on the ground, the moonlight revealing the ghastly scene.

Officer Harris smirked, his eyes gleaming with a twisted satisfaction. "Looks like you stumbled upon something you shouldn't have, kids."

Cole's heart pounded in his chest, a mixture of dread and disbelief flooding his senses. They had walked right into a trap, and now an innocent life had been taken. The realization of the darkness lurking within Dupo weighed heavily upon him, threatening to crush his spirit.

Maya, her voice trembling, spoke with a mix of anger and fear. "You... you monster! What have you done?"

Officer Harris chuckled, a cold, chilling sound that sent shivers down their spines. "This town needs order, and sometimes sacrifices must be made. You're next."

With a sudden surge of adrenaline, Cole and Maya turned and ran, their hearts pounding in their ears. Scraps barked and followed closely at their heels. They fled into the labyrinth of alleyways, their only goal to escape the clutches of the corrupt police officer.

As they ran, fear and determination intertwined within their souls. They knew they couldn't let Officer Harris continue his reign of terror, but they also realized they needed to uncover the truth behind the ghostly entity and its connection to the darkness that plagued Dupo.

Desperation led them to seek refuge in an old abandoned warehouse on the outskirts of town. Its dilapidated walls and broken windows whispered tales of forgotten dreams and hidden secrets. The trio huddled together, catching their breath and contemplating their next move.

Scraps, ever the loyal companion, sniffed the air and began to growl, his hackles raised. His canine instincts sensed an imminent danger, one that lurked in the shadows, unseen but undeniably present.

Cole's eyes widened as he noticed a flicker of movement in the corner of the room. A pair of haunting eyes peered at them from the darkness. It was the ghostly entity, its ethereal form taking shape once again. Its presence seemed stronger, as if fueled by the sorrow and desperation that pervaded the town.

With a sense of urgency, Cole and Maya approached the ghostly figure, their voices filled with determination. "We need your help. Help us uncover the truth, and together, we can put an end to the darkness that haunts Dupo."

The ghostly entity hesitated for a moment before nodding in agreement. It beckoned them to follow, and as they moved deeper into the warehouse, the truth began to unfold before their eyes.

They discovered a hidden chamber beneath the warehouse floor, a forgotten catacomb of secrets. Within its dimly lit confines, they found journals, photographs, and documents that revealed a web of corruption, covering up Officer Harris's heinous acts. They also uncovered the ghost's true identity—a victim of Harris's reign of terror, seeking justice from beyond the grave.

Driven by a newfound purpose, Cole, Maya, Scraps, and the ghostly entity set out to expose the truth and bring justice to Dupo. They would face unimaginable dangers and confront the depths of human depravity, but they were determined to restore the soul of their town.

As they stepped back into the moonlit night, shadows lengthening behind them, the battle lines were drawn. The final act had begun, and in the heart of Dupo, a dance of light and darkness would unfold, leading to a confrontation that would determine the fate of not only the artists and musicians but the very essence of the town itself.

Chapter 4: Whispers of the Bluffs

As the night cloaked the town of Dupo, Cole, Maya, Scraps, and the ghostly entity found themselves standing at the edge of a desolate bluff overlooking the expanse of the town. In the pale moonlight, the silhouette of the bluffs appeared both majestic and foreboding, their rocky formations towering like ancient sentinels.

Guided by the ghostly entity, they descended a hidden path, winding their way through the dense foliage that clung to the bluff's edge. The air grew damp and heavy as they entered a concealed entrance that led deep into the bowels of the earth. The walls of the cave whispered secrets, their echoes carrying the weight of forgotten stories.

The path through the cave twisted and turned, leading them deeper into the underground labyrinth. They treaded carefully, their footsteps punctuated by the occasional drip of water from stalactites above. The sound echoed eerily, resonating through the narrow passages like a haunting melody.

Cole's heart quickened with each step, his anticipation mixed with trepidation. He wondered what mysteries awaited them in the depths of these interconnected caves. The legends whispered by the townsfolk spoke of a hidden power within these ancient caverns, an energy that had drawn evil forces to Dupo.

As they pressed forward, the walls of the cave gave way to a vast underground chamber. The glow of their flashlights danced across the stalagmites and stalactites, casting eerie shadows on the cavern walls. It was a sight that both mesmerized and unnerved them.

Within this hidden realm, they stumbled upon faded markings on the cave walls. Symbols and drawings told stories of long-forgotten rituals, hinting at a dark history intertwined with Dupo's very foundation. The ghostly entity, emanating an ethereal glow, seemed to recognize these symbols and led them deeper into the depths.

  Their journey through the interconnected cave system brought them to a subterranean river that flowed beneath the town. Its dark waters glistened under the faint light, reflecting the weight of the secrets it held. Cole's mind whirled with thoughts of how these caves and the river connected to the bluffs above, forming a complex network that seemed to entwine with the very fabric of Dupo.

They followed the river's course, wading through ankle-deep water, their senses heightened by the sound of rushing currents echoing off the walls. The deeper they ventured, the more the air grew heavy, as if the cave itself exhaled a collective breath, hinting at the darkness that lay ahead.

Finally, they reached an underground chamber that stood at the heart of the cave system. The ghostly entity halted, its form flickering with a mix of anticipation and sadness. As Cole and Maya approached, they could feel the presence of an ancient evil lurking in the shadows, ready to unleash its malevolence upon the town above.

A voice whispered through the chamber, cold and chilling. "You have come far, but the price for meddling in these affairs is steep. Prepare to face the consequences."

Suddenly, the darkness coalesced into a tangible form. A monstrous figure emerged from the shadows, its eyes gleaming with malice. It was a creature born of the cave's darkness, an embodiment of the accumulated sorrow and wickedness that had seeped into the very bedrock of Dupo.

Cole, Maya, Scraps, and the ghostly entity stood their ground, their resolve unwavering. They were prepared to face this ancient evil, knowing that their town's salvation hung in the balance. With hearts brimming with courage, they prepared to confront the horrors that awaited them within the depths of the underground chamber.

The final battle had begun, with the fate of Dupo resting upon their shoulders. The bluffs and the interconnected caves whispered tales of forgotten power, and now it was up to this determined group to silence the darkness and restore balance to their town.

Chapter 5: Shadows Unleashed

The air in the underground chamber grew heavy with anticipation as Cole, Maya, Scraps, and the ghostly entity faced the monstrous figure born of darkness. Its presence loomed over them, a palpable manifestation of the malevolence that had plagued Dupo.

Officer Harris, driven by his wicked ambitions, stood at the creature's side, a twisted ally in its dark endeavors. The glimmer of malice in his eyes spoke volumes, his intentions aligned with the very forces that threatened to devour the town.

Cole locked eyes with Officer Harris, a mixture of anger and determination fueling his gaze. He knew that the corrupt officer held the key to the town's suffering, and justice demanded that he pay for his crimes. But before Cole could confront him, the ghostly entity stepped forward, radiating an ethereal power that seemed to draw strength from the depths of the cave.

A whisper echoed through the chamber, the voice of the ghostly entity carrying a weight of sorrow and vengeance. "Officer Harris, your reign of darkness ends here. Your crimes against this town will no longer go unpunished."

Officer Harris sneered, his arrogance faltering ever so slightly. "You think you can stop me? You're nothing but a ghost, a mere specter of the past."

With a surge of ethereal energy, the ghostly entity lunged forward, its incorporeal form passing through Officer Harris. A chilling cry escaped his lips as his body contorted in agony, wracked by the invisible grip of the ghost's wrath. The malevolent officer fell to the ground, his life extinguished by the very darkness he had embraced.

The monstrous figure, enraged by the loss of its ally, roared in fury. Its massive form thrashed within the confines of the underground chamber, sending tremors through the cave system. Rocks tumbled from the ceiling, and the ground shook beneath their feet. Yet, Cole, Maya, Scraps, and the ghostly entity stood their ground, united in their resolve to vanquish the ancient evil.

In a surge of courage and determination, Cole and Maya channeled their creative energy, their artistic souls fueling their actions. They painted symbols and glyphs on the cave walls, calling upon the power of light and creativity to combat the darkness. Their vibrant colors clashed with the shadows, forming a barrier of hope that shielded them from the creature's onslaught.

The battle raged on, a dance of light and darkness, of determination and malevolence. The ground quaked, and the air crackled with power as they fought to tip the scales in favor of Dupo's salvation.

As the creature's strength waned, weakened by the relentless assault, the ghostly entity joined the final skirmish. With a surge of ethereal energy, it lashed out, wrapping its ghostly tendrils around the ancient evil. The creature let out a bone-chilling shriek as the combined forces of light and ghostly vengeance consumed it, banishing it from the depths of the cave forever.

Exhausted but triumphant, Cole, Maya, Scraps, and the ghostly entity emerged from the underground chamber, blinking in the dim light of the cave's exit. Above them, the bluffs stood sentinel, their rocky forms bathed in the gentle glow of dawn. It was a new day for Dupo, a dawn of hope and redemption.

The town of Dupo would forever bear the scars of its dark past, but the artists, musicians, and the resilient spirits of its inhabitants would heal its wounds and bring life back to its streets. The ghosts of the past would find solace in the embrace of a town reborn, and the legends of its haunted caves would become whispered tales of resilience and triumph.

And so, Cole, Maya, Scraps, and the ghostly entity made their way back to the surface, ready to face the challenges that awaited them. The horrors that once plagued Dupo had been laid to rest, and a newfound sense of unity and creative power infused the town.

As the sun broke through the clouds, casting its warm rays upon the streets of Dupo, a vibrant tapestry of art, music, and the resilient spirit of its people unfurled. The legacy of the ghostly entity and the battles fought in the depths of the caves would forever be etched in the hearts and minds of those who dared to dream and believe in the power of light amidst the shadows.

Dupo would rise again, a testament to the indomitable spirit of its residents, forever intertwined with the echoes of the bluffs and the secrets of the interconnected caves.

Chapter 6: A New Dawn

In the aftermath of the battle that banished the darkness from Dupo's depths, a sense of transformation swept through the town. The residents felt a renewed hope, and the artists and musicians found their voices amplified, their creations shining with a vibrant energy that reverberated through the streets.

As the sun cast its warm rays upon Dupo, a new police officer arrived, bearing a badge of honor and a determination to serve the community. Officer Elena Ramirez, a compassionate and fair-minded individual, understood the challenges the town faced and was committed to upholding justice and fostering a sense of safety.

Officer Ramirez wasted no time in forging connections with the town's artists, musicians, and residents. She recognized their invaluable contributions and sought to bridge the gap between law enforcement and the creative spirits that breathed life into Dupo's streets. Together, they formed a united front against the remnants of darkness that still lingered.

Under Officer Ramirez's guidance, the town witnessed a decline in drug use and theft. Her presence and dedication to community policing fostered an atmosphere of trust, allowing residents to come forward with information and concerns. Through collaboration and open communication, they worked together to restore a sense of harmony to Dupo.

The artists and musicians flourished under Officer Ramirez's support. Their talents were embraced and celebrated, transforming the town's walls into vibrant murals that told stories of resilience, unity, and hope. Graffiti artists, once regarded as outlaws, found themselves recognized as catalysts for positive change, their work breathing life into forgotten corners of Dupo.

The dark forces that had plagued Dupo seemed to have dissipated, their influence overshadowed by the power of creativity and a community united in purpose. The stories of the haunted caves and the battles fought within them became a part of the town's folklore, a testament to its resilience and the triumph of the human spirit.

As the years passed, Dupo thrived under the watchful eye of Officer Ramirez and the collective efforts of its residents. The town became a beacon of creativity, attracting artists, musicians, and dreamers from far and wide. Its streets pulsed with life, its walls adorned with masterpieces that showcased the town's vibrant soul.

The legacy of the ghostly entity remained imprinted in the hearts of those who had witnessed the battle between light and darkness. Its presence served as a reminder of the fragility of balance and the importance of nurturing the bonds of community.

In the end, Dupo became a symbol of transformation—a testament to the power of unity, art, and a new generation of leaders like Officer Ramirez. The echoes of its dark past mingled with the whispers of hope and resilience, forever etching their mark on the fabric of the town.

As the sun set on Dupo, casting a warm golden glow over its streets, the spirit of the town remained untamed, continuing to inspire generations to come. It stood as a testament to the indomitable human spirit and the capacity for change, reminding the world that even in the face of darkness, a new dawn is always within reach.

Epilogue: A Transformed Dupo

Years had passed since the final battle that banished the darkness from Dupo's streets. The town had undergone a remarkable transformation, its spirit revitalized, its residents united in a newfound harmony. The legacy of the past had become an indelible mark on Dupo's collective memory, a testament to the resilience and triumph of the human spirit.

Cole, once a troubled graffiti artist, had found solace in the aftermath of the battles that had shaped his destiny. He continued to create art that reflected the newfound light and hope within the town, inspiring others to embrace their creativity and defy the shadows that had once consumed them.

Officer Ramirez, the compassionate and fair-minded police officer, had become a beacon of trust and justice in Dupo. Her commitment to serving the community, alongside the support of fellow officers who shared her values, had paved the way for a new era of law enforcement in the town.

The specter of Officer Harris had been laid to rest, his darkness vanquished forever. His demise had served as a warning, a reminder that corruption could be overcome, and that the pursuit of justice required unwavering dedication and integrity.

With the darkness lifted, the town experienced a renaissance of creativity and community. Artists and musicians thrived, their expressions of art reverberating through the streets, painting a tapestry of vibrancy and unity. The walls of Dupo became a living gallery, showcasing the stories, dreams, and emotions of its residents.

Graffiti artists, once regarded as outlaws, were now celebrated as guardians of the town's spirit, their murals and tags adding a touch of colorful rebellion to the urban landscape. Music filled the air, from impromptu jam sessions on street corners to lively performances in local venues, breathing life into the soul of Dupo.

The bluffs that overlooked the town stood as silent witnesses to the transformation that had taken place. The interconnected caves, once a realm of shadows and mystery, had become a symbol of resilience and the power of collective strength. They remained an ever-present reminder of the battles fought and the triumphs won, etching their mark on the fabric of Dupo's history.

As the sun dipped below the horizon, casting a warm glow over the town, the residents of Dupo gathered for a celebration—an expression of gratitude and joy for the healing that had taken place. Laughter echoed through the streets, mingling with the melodies of music, as the spirit of unity and creativity thrived.

In the epilogue of Dupo's story, the whispers of darkness had been silenced, replaced by the harmonious cadence of a town reborn. The journey of Cole, Officer Ramirez, and the resilient inhabitants of Dupo had come full circle, leaving behind a legacy of redemption and inspiration.

And so, as the moon rose in the night sky, casting its gentle glow over Dupo, the town embraced its future with open arms. The lessons learned and the battles fought had left an indomitable mark on the hearts and minds of its residents, forever transforming Dupo into a beacon of light and artistic expression.

The End

Made in United States
Troutdale, OR
07/18/2023